ISBN: 0-439-53849-1

Shrek is a registered trademark of DreamWorks L.L.C. Shrek 2, Shrek Ears,
and Shrek "S" Design TM and © 2004 DreamWorks L.L.C.
Published by Scholastic Inc.
SCHOLASTIC and associated logos are trademarks and/or registered trademarks of Scholastic Inc.

12 11 10 9 8 7 6 5 4 3 2 1   4 5 6 7 8/0

Printed in the U.S.A.
First printing, May 2004

SHREK 2™

THE MOVIE STORYBOOK

Adaptation by
Tom Mason and Dan Danko
Illustration by Koelsch Studios

SCHOLASTIC INC.

New York   Toronto   London   Auckland   Sydney
Mexico City   New Delhi   Hong Kong   Buenos Aires

Once upon a time in the land of Far Far Away, there lived a King and a Queen. They were blessed with a beautiful baby girl. But every night, when the sun went down, their beautiful baby girl turned into a not-so-beautiful baby ogre.

They did what any parent would do with an ogre child — they locked her away in a tower to await the kiss of a very handsome prince. Prince Charming, in fact.

However, when Prince Charming entered the tallest room of the tallest tower, he discovered that Princess Fiona had gone on her honeymoon with someone else.

At least that's what the Wolf said. He was there waiting instead of Fiona.

Shrek and Fiona returned from their honeymoon to the swamp. But instead of peace and quiet, they found Donkey and a royal page.

The page carried a scroll, which he unrolled and started reading.

"Dearest Fiona . . . we are so thrilled you finally found your 'Happily Ever After.' Please join us in the kingdom of Far Far Away for a royal ball in honor of your marriage. We can't wait to meet your . . . Prince Charming."

Shrek smiled and gave a small finger-wave.

"Love, Mum and Dad . . . " the page finished.

"Mum and Dad?" Fiona gasped.

"Prince Charming?" Shrek gasped and looked at Fiona.

"Royal ball?" said Donkey. "I love a party!"

"We're not going!" Shrek yelled. But then he looked at Fiona and realized they just might.

Through the woods, along winding roads, over mountains and bridges the onion carriage traveled toward Far Far Away.

"Are we there yet?" Donkey asked.

They plodded alongside rivers, through tunnels, and around lakes.

"Are we there yet?" he asked again and again.

"This is taking forever, Shrek!" Donkey pleaded. "I'm really bored."

"Well, find a way to entertain yourself," Shrek muttered.

For a few moments, the carriage was silent.

"Pop!" Donkey said.

Donkey looked at Shrek and Fiona, then out the window and at the floor.

"Pop!"

Shrek and Fiona sank in their seats.

"Pop!"

Shrek put his head in his hands.

"Pop!"

"Arrgghhh!" Shrek couldn't take it. "For five minutes, could you not be yourself, Donkey?"

"Pop!" Donkey replied.

"Arrrggghhh! Are we there yet?" cried Shrek.

Fiona gasped excitedly as she glanced out her window. "Yes!"

The kingdom of Far Far Away was beautiful. In fact, it was the most beautiful place in any land near or far. It was where fairy-tale folk went to live Happily Ever After.

"We are definitely not in the swamp anymore," Shrek commented as the onion carriage passed fancy shops, gorgeous mansions, and beautiful townspeople. Finally they stopped in front of the King and Queen's castle.

A large crowd had gathered. A long red carpet was unrolled. A servant opened the carriage door. Beautiful white doves were released into the air.

Shrek stepped from the carriage and the crowd gasped in horror. The trumpets died down. The crowd grew silent.

Donkey stepped backward into the carriage. "Why don't you guys go ahead? I'll park the car." The carriage quietly drove off as Shrek and Fiona stood nervously on the red carpet.

"Now let's go home before they light the torches," Shrek said.

CRUNCH! That night, Shrek popped an escargot into his mouth, chewing the shell loudly.

"So, Fiona, tell us about your new home," the King finally said.

"Shrek owns his own land, Daddy."

"Oh, yes," Shrek said. "It's in an enchanted forest, with lots of squirrels and cute little duckies . . . "

"Don't tell me you're talking about the swamp!" Donkey interrupted.

"A swamp," the King said. "An ogre from the swamp. How original."

Before Shrek could answer, the doors flew open and waiters entered carrying tray after tray of royal delicacies.

The King reached for a large lobster and pulled it toward him.

"I suppose that any grandchildren I could expect would be —"

"Ogres," said Shrek. He grabbed a baked pig.

"Not that there's anything wrong with that," the Queen urged. "Right, Harold?"

The King ripped open the lobster shell. "Of course not. Assuming you don't eat your young."

Fiona looked embarrassed. "Dad . . . "

Shrek tore off a pig leg and took a bite. "No, we usually lock our kids away in a tower."

"Shrek!" Fiona said.

"I did what was best for her," the King said.

"Stop it! Both of you!" Fiona cried as she ran from the table while the King and Shrek glared angrily at each other.

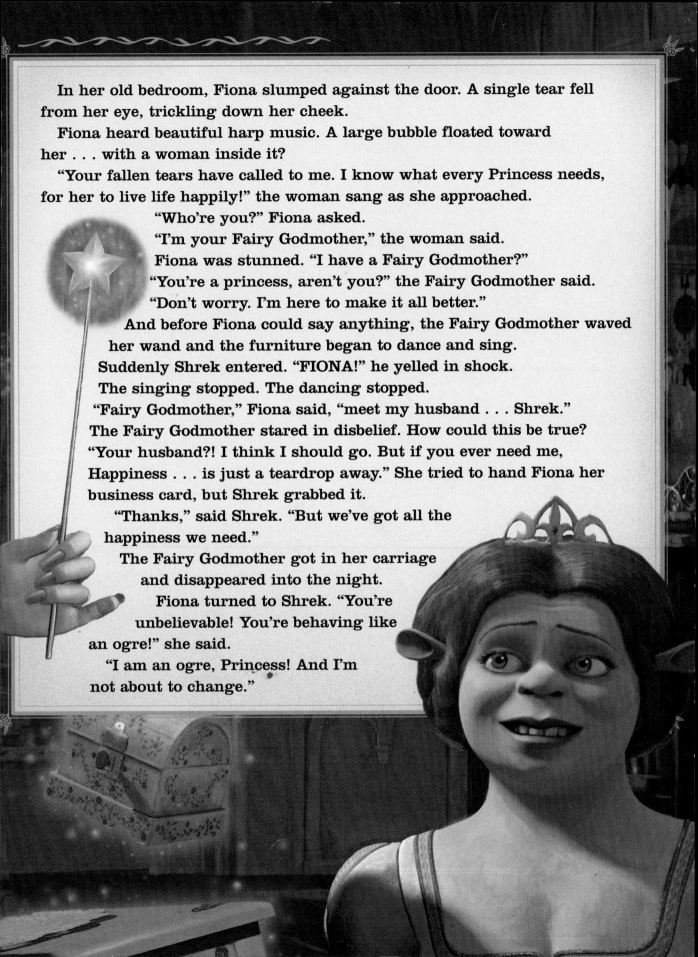

In her old bedroom, Fiona slumped against the door. A single tear fell from her eye, trickling down her cheek.

Fiona heard beautiful harp music. A large bubble floated toward her . . . with a woman inside it?

"Your fallen tears have called to me. I know what every Princess needs, for her to live life happily!" the woman sang as she approached.

"Who're you?" Fiona asked.

"I'm your Fairy Godmother," the woman said.

Fiona was stunned. "I have a Fairy Godmother?"

"You're a princess, aren't you?" the Fairy Godmother said. "Don't worry. I'm here to make it all better."

And before Fiona could say anything, the Fairy Godmother waved her wand and the furniture began to dance and sing.

Suddenly Shrek entered. "FIONA!" he yelled in shock.

The singing stopped. The dancing stopped.

"Fairy Godmother," Fiona said, "meet my husband . . . Shrek."

The Fairy Godmother stared in disbelief. How could this be true? "Your husband?! I think I should go. But if you ever need me, Happiness . . . is just a teardrop away." She tried to hand Fiona her business card, but Shrek grabbed it.

"Thanks," said Shrek. "But we've got all the happiness we need."

The Fairy Godmother got in her carriage and disappeared into the night.

Fiona turned to Shrek. "You're unbelievable! You're behaving like an ogre!" she said.

"I am an ogre, Princess! And I'm not about to change."

Later that night, the King, the Fairy Godmother, and Prince Charming sat in the carriage outside the Friar's Fat Boy restaurant.

"Comfy?" the Fairy Godmother asked. She wanted to know why Fiona was married to an ogre — and not to her son, Prince Charming. The King tried to explain that it wasn't his fault, but the Fairy Godmother wasn't listening.

After all, she said, Prince Charming had done what he was supposed to do: endure blistering winds and scorching deserts, climb to the top of the tallest tower . . . so what went wrong?

"It wasn't my fault," the King defended.

"We made a deal, Harold, and you don't want me to go back on my part."

"No," the King said, suddenly very nervous.

"So Fiona and Charming will be together?" the Fairy Godmother asked as she unwrapped her Renaissance Wrap.

"Yes, but — what am I supposed to do about it?" asked the King.

"The ogre's in the way, Harold. Lose him!" the Fairy Godmother demanded as she flew away in her coach.

A rundown pub called The Poison Apple stood at the edge of the kingdom.

The disguised King entered. "Excuse me," he said to the bartender. "I need to speak to someone," the King stuttered, "about an ogre."

"There's only one fellow who can handle a job like that," the bartender said, pointing to a door in the back of The Poison Apple.

"Hello . . . ?" the King called out timidly, walking into a dark room.

"Who dares to enter my room?"

"I was told that you were the one to talk to about — "

"Yes, an ogre," a voice said. "For this I charge a great deal of money."

The King took out a heavy sack and threw it on the table. Gold coins spilled out.

"You have engaged my services. Tell me where I can find this ogre," the mysterious voice purred.

Shrek couldn't sleep. He paced the floor of Fiona's room, then opened her old hope chest. Inside, he found her old diary. He flipped through the pages and started reading.

He read about Fiona's childhood. She wrote about how her parents never let her go out at night. Then they told her that she was going away — to school she thought, but Shrek knew that it was to the tower from which he'd rescued her. Most of all, however, the book was filled with pages about Fiona's future with her husband, Prince Charming. It made Shrek feel very sad.

Suddenly he heard a noise from outside. Footsteps and a knock at the door! He slammed the diary shut.

Fiona was still sleeping, as Shrek opened the door.

"I hope I'm not interrupting anything," said the King, standing in the doorway.

"Uh, I was just reading a scary book," Shrek said.

"I was hoping you'd let me apologize for my behavior earlier," the King began. Then he invited Shrek to join him for a morning hunt.

Shrek hesitated, but the King pulled out his ace.

"I know it would mean the world to Fiona," he said.

Shrek took one look at Fiona, and knew what he was doing in the morning. Hunting.

The next morning, Shrek and Donkey walked through the woods. After several hours, Shrek had to admit the obvious. They were lost.

"We can't be lost, Shrek," said Donkey. "We followed the king's instructions exactly. Isn't this the 'deepest, darkest part of the woods'?"

Shrek agreed. The woods were deep and dark.

"Okay," Donkey admitted. "We're lost."

"That's what I've been saying. And stop that purring."

"I'm not purring," Donkey said. "Donkeys don't purr."

"Fear me, if you dare! Hisss! Hisss!" a voice suddenly cried from behind them.

Shrek and Donkey turned. The purring creature — whatever it was — was wearing leather boots, a feathered, floppy musketeer hat, and wielding a sword.

"Hey, look, a little cat," Shrek said.

"Look out, Shrek! He's armed!" Donkey yelled, staring at the cat's sword.

Puss In Boots leaped out of his boots and dove at Shrek, claws extended.

"YEE-OWWW!" Shrek screamed. "Get it off! Get it off! Bad kitty!"

"Hold on, Shrek! I'm coming!" Donkey yelled.

Donkey let loose a thunderous kick, smacking Shrek. Shrek doubled over in pain as Puss leaped off, jumped through the air, and landed back in his boots. He snapped his hat back on and drew his sword, carving a "P" into a nearby tree.

"Now, ye ogre, beg for mercy from . . . Puss . . . In Boots!"

Puss started to laugh. Then cough. Then cough even louder. He dropped his sword and fell to his knees, wheezing, choking, and gasping for breath. Just when it sounded like it would never stop, he finally coughed up a hairball.

"That is nasty," Donkey said.

Shrek grabbed the helpless cat by the scruff of his neck and lifted him off the ground. "What'ya reckon we should do with him, Donkey?"

"No, por favor!" Puss interrupted. "It was nothing personal to you, señor. It's just that the King offered so much in gold and I have a litter of brothers — "

"Whoa! Hold on!" Shrek was astonished. "Fiona's father paid you to get rid of me?"

"Sí," Puss admitted.

Shrek reached into his pants and pulled out the Fairy Godmother's business card. "Are you up for a little quest, Donkey?" Shrek asked.

"All right!" Donkey cheered. "Shrek and Donkey on another whirlwind adventure!!"

"Stop!" Puss shouted. "On my honor I, Puss In Boots, am obliged to accompany you until I have saved your life as you have spared mine."

Donkey galloped in front of Puss. "Sorry, the position of annoying talking animal has already been taken."

"C'mon, Donkey," Shrek said. "Look at him, in his wee little boots. Let's keep him."

Shrek, Donkey, and Puss In Boots went to see the Fairy Godmother but she refused to help them. In fact, she laughed when Shrek said he wanted to be a handsome prince. But Shrek wasn't giving up . . . he had a plan.

"Man, you sure this is gonna work?" Donkey's voice echoed in the hallway.

"Shhh," Shrek shushed as they approached the potion room.

Inside the room, shelves ran from the floor to the ceiling. Each was filled with hundreds of different potions, magic formulas, and secret sauces, all in tiny bottles.

"One of these has got to help," Shrek said.

Shrek pointed Puss toward the shelves. Puss jumped up and started prowling around.

"How about Happily Ever After?" Puss said. "It says 'beauty divine.'"

"That's the one."

Puss grabbed the potion bottle, but the bottle slipped from his paw and fell toward the floor. Just in time, Donkey dove, and caught the bottle in his mouth.

But then an alarm went off and lights began flashing; a heavy security gate started to descend in front of the door — and Donkey swallowed the bottle! Shrek grabbed Puss and Donkey and they slid under the gate just before it came crashing down.

Two armed elves ran toward Shrek, their crossbows ready. Shrek grabbed Donkey and Puss and cartwheeled away as the arrows flew past.

As he reached a bubbling cauldron, Shrek pushed it over. Boiling potion spilled onto the factory floor.

Potion washed over the guards and the test animals in their cages. Elves and animals suddenly began turning into doves.

Meanwhile, Shrek leaped up into the air and grabbed hold of a hook on a pulley. Swinging his legs, he propelled himself, Donkey, and Puss across the length of the factory. When Shrek reached the end of the cable, he let go and, as they landed, the bottle of potion popped out of Donkey's mouth. Shrek scooped it up and the three ran off into the forest.

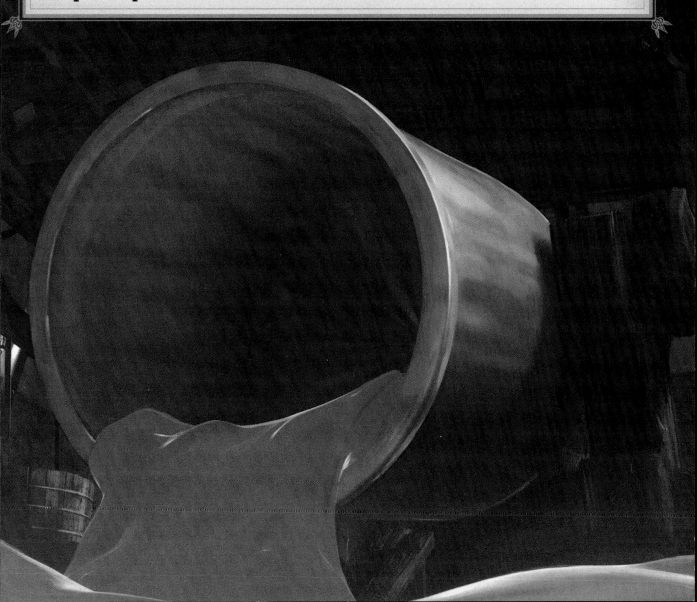

In the forest, Shrek pulled out the potion bottle. "Happily Ever After," he read. "Maximum strength. For you and your true love."

"Allow me to take the first sip, Boss," Puss offered. "It would be an honor to lay my life on the line for you."

Donkey pushed Puss aside. "No, no, no!" Donkey said. "If there's gonna be any animal testing, that's the best friend's job. Gimme that bottle."

Donkey grabbed the bottle from Shrek and took a big gulp. "Aah!" he said, wiping his chin. He stood, waiting. Shrek and Puss stared at him for a long time. "I don't feel any different," Donkey commented. "Do I look any different?"

"Maybe it doesn't work on Donkeys." Shrek held the bottle up. "Here's to us, Fiona!" He guzzled down the liquid.

In the sky above, storm clouds gathered, a cold wind blew, thunder rumbled . . . and nothing happened. Except Shrek farted.

"Maybe Fiona and I were never meant to be happy," Shrek said sadly.

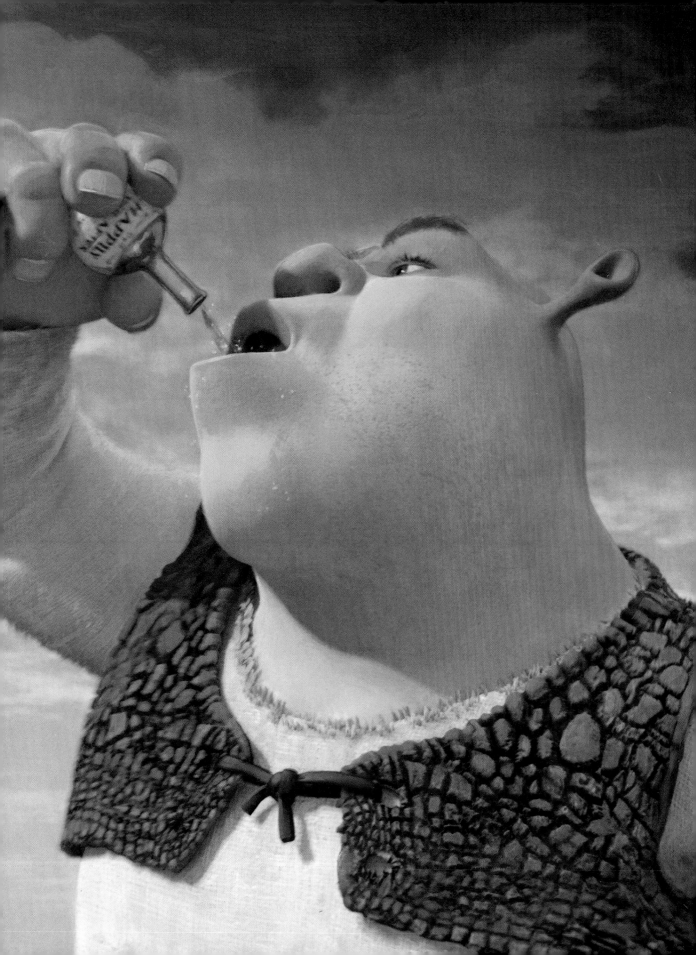

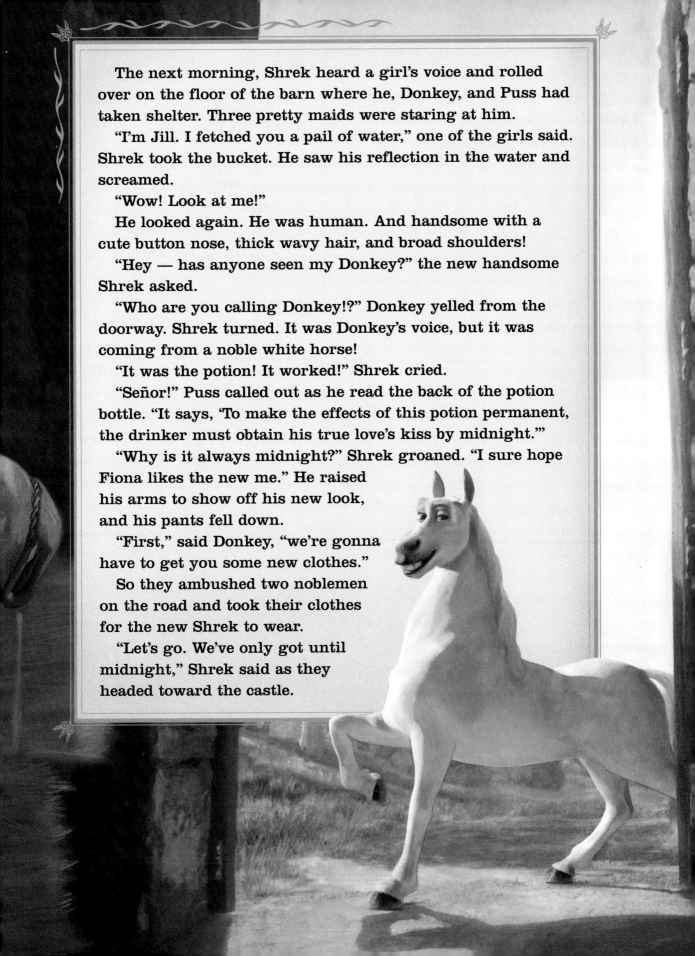

The next morning, Shrek heard a girl's voice and rolled over on the floor of the barn where he, Donkey, and Puss had taken shelter. Three pretty maids were staring at him.

"I'm Jill. I fetched you a pail of water," one of the girls said. Shrek took the bucket. He saw his reflection in the water and screamed.

"Wow! Look at me!"

He looked again. He was human. And handsome with a cute button nose, thick wavy hair, and broad shoulders!

"Hey — has anyone seen my Donkey?" the new handsome Shrek asked.

"Who are you calling Donkey!?" Donkey yelled from the doorway. Shrek turned. It was Donkey's voice, but it was coming from a noble white horse!

"It was the potion! It worked!" Shrek cried.

"Señor!" Puss called out as he read the back of the potion bottle. "It says, 'To make the effects of this potion permanent, the drinker must obtain his true love's kiss by midnight.'"

"Why is it always midnight?" Shrek groaned. "I sure hope Fiona likes the new me." He raised his arms to show off his new look, and his pants fell down.

"First," said Donkey, "we're gonna have to get you some new clothes."

So they ambushed two noblemen on the road and took their clothes for the new Shrek to wear.

"Let's go. We've only got until midnight," Shrek said as they headed toward the castle.

The potion also had an effect on Fiona. That same morning she woke up, and went to the sink to wash her face. She dried off with a towel and then looked in the mirror. She was beautiful.

She screamed.

As he approached the castle, Shrek heard her. "Fiona!" he shouted and ran toward her room.

But when he entered he saw the Fairy Godmother.

With a small wave of her magic wand, the furniture slid in front of the door and Shrek was trapped.

Fiona ran downstairs, calling Shrek's name. In the main hall, she saw Prince Charming — handsome, amazing, wonderful, and, of course, charming.

"Shrek?" she gasped, smiling at him.

"The potion changed a lot of things," Prince Charming lied, "but not the way I feel about you."

From the balcony in the room, Shrek watched as Fiona and her parents embraced Prince Charming.

"Such a handsome couple, don't you agree?" asked the Fairy Godmother. "She's finally found the Prince of her dreams. Something you'll never be."

"I only wanted to make her happy," Shrek said. He could feel his new handsome heart breaking. "That's all I ever wanted."

"You're an ogre," the Fairy Godmother reminded him. "Quit living in a fairy tale and go back to the swamp where you belong."

Shrek headed toward the door. Maybe he did belong in the swamp after all.

"Here you go, boys," the Ugly Stepsister said, plopping glasses down on the counter at The Poison Apple.

Shrek, Donkey, and Puss sat alone at the bar.

"It was all a mistake," Shrek said sadly. "I never should have rescued Fiona from that tower."

"I can't believe you're just gonna walk away," Donkey said.
"But she's in love with Prince Charming," Shrek sighed.
"Shrek, you love Fiona," Donkey said.
He did. But Shrek was convinced that Fiona — as well as her parents — would be happier if she married Prince Charming.

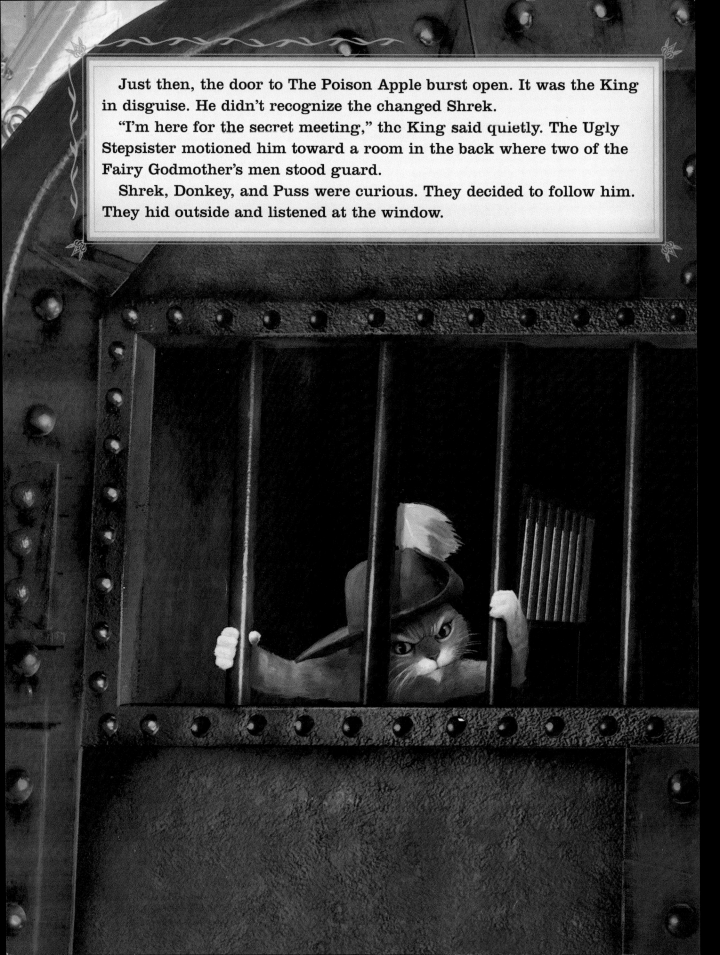

Just then, the door to The Poison Apple burst open. It was the King in disguise. He didn't recognize the changed Shrek.

"I'm here for the secret meeting," the King said quietly. The Ugly Stepsister motioned him toward a room in the back where two of the Fairy Godmother's men stood guard.

Shrek, Donkey, and Puss were curious. They decided to follow him. They hid outside and listened at the window.

Inside the room, the King was explaining to the Fairy Godmother and Prince Charming that their plan wasn't working. Fiona wasn't falling in love with the Prince. The King thought that they should just forget the whole plan. But the Fairy Godmother did not agree, and she reminded the King that he had to help her or else . . .

Suddenly there was a noise from outside. The Fairy Godmother looked at the window. She recognized Shrek. She had an idea.

"Thieves! Stop them!" she cried, knowing her guards would capture him.

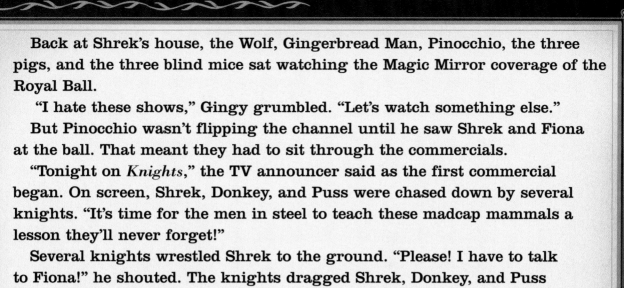

Back at Shrek's house, the Wolf, Gingerbread Man, Pinocchio, the three pigs, and the three blind mice sat watching the Magic Mirror coverage of the Royal Ball.

"I hate these shows," Gingy grumbled. "Let's watch something else."

But Pinocchio wasn't flipping the channel until he saw Shrek and Fiona at the ball. That meant they had to sit through the commercials.

"Tonight on *Knights*," the TV announcer said as the first commercial began. On screen, Shrek, Donkey, and Puss were chased down by several knights. "It's time for the men in steel to teach these madcap mammals a lesson they'll never forget!"

Several knights wrestled Shrek to the ground. "Please! I have to talk to Fiona!" he shouted. The knights dragged Shrek, Donkey, and Puss into the paddy wagon and slammed the door shut, locking it with a mighty KLANG!

"I'm her husband!" Shrek yelled, but nobody listened. Except for the Wolf, Gingerbread Man, Pinocchio, the three pigs, and the three blind mice. They heard it all.

Shrek, Donkey, and Puss were chained to the wall of a prison cell.

"How long have we been here? I can't take it anymore! I've gotta get out of here!" Donkey shouted.

"Donkey, you have the right to remain silent," Shrek said.

"And the sooner the better," Puss added, "before I go totally mad."

"Hey!" a voice cried from above. They looked up and saw Pinocchio and Gingy staring down at them through a grate in the ceiling. "We've come to get you out!"

BOOM! The lock on the ceiling grate blew off. The three pigs lowered Pinocchio by his puppet strings into the cell.

But Pinocchio couldn't reach.

"Quick! Tell a lie," Gingy said as he slid down and landed on Pinocchio's nose.

"I cannot tell a lie," Pinocchio replied. And that was a lie. His nose grew, inching Gingy closer to Shrek so he could grab Shrek's shackles and unlock them.

"Now we can storm the castle and rescue the fair princess!" Puss proclaimed.

"Gingy, do you still know where the Muffin Man lives?" Shrek asked.

"Sure! Down on Drury Lane," the Gingerbread Man answered. "Why?"

"We're going to need flour. Lots and lots of flour," Shrek said.

"Ladies and gentlemen, I give you Princess Fiona and her new husband, Shrek!"

Fiona and Prince Charming entered the ball. As they walked down the stairs, the Prince waved to the crowd.

"What are you doing?" Fiona asked.

"I'm just playing the part, Fiona. The people love waving. You look radiant, darling." He leaned in for a kiss.

"Is that glitter on your lips?" Fiona asked.

"Cherry flavored."

Fiona shook her head in disgust as they reached the final stair. The crowd started to chant: "Dance . . . dance . . . dance."

Prince Charming looked at Fiona and took her hand. She couldn't say no.

"Since when do you dance?" Fiona asked.

"Love is full of surprises," Prince Charming said.

THUMP. THUMP. THUMP.

Giant footsteps echoed toward the castle. From over the hill came a giant gingerbread man. Shrek held onto the giant cookie's shoulders while Donkey and Puss rode behind.

"Let's go, Mongo," Shrek shouted at the giant cookie.

As they got closer to the castle, a screaming ball of fire flew right at Mongo. The guards were attacking with catapults and fireballs.

A fireball hit Mongo, knocking off one of his gumdrop buttons. Now he was mad! He kicked the button, sending it back over the castle walls. WHAM! It destroyed the catapults!

As they reached the castle gates, Mongo pulled on the doors. Pulling, pulling, with all his giant cookie might, the gates started to give.

But the guards had a secret weapon — they poured milk into a hot cauldron and dumped the steaming liquid onto the giant gingerbread man. Mongo's arms broke off, wedged between the doors.

The giant cookie man fell backward into the moat as Shrek leaped through the crack in the doors.

Seconds later, the drawbridge lowered. Donkey, Puss, Gingy, and the rest of the fairy-tale creatures ran across.

"Back away from my wife!" Shrek shouted at Prince Charming as he arrived at the ballroom.

Fiona was amazed. This was Shrek? But then who was she dancing with?

The Fairy Godmother was furious. She raised her wand and aimed it at Shrek, but the fairy-tale folk rushed into action. One of the three pigs flew at the Fairy Godmother while Pinocchio grabbed her wand. But a spell turned him into a real boy and he dropped the wand again.

One of the pigs snatched the wand and threw it to Donkey. The Fairy Godmother chased after him. Donkey threw the wand to Gingy who tossed it to the three blind mice. They missed it. A blast of magic turned Pinocchio back into a puppet.

The wand skittered across the floor, but before the Fairy Godmother could reach it, Puss In Boots flipped the wand up in the air with his sword and caught it.

Now the Fairy Godmother was really mad. She stretched out her hand. The magic wand wiggled and jerked, then flew back to her.

"You couldn't just go back to your swamp," she hissed at Shrek.

The Fairy Godmother summoned all of her powers. A blast of magic roared from the wand. Shrek pushed Fiona out of the way, prepared to take the blast himself. But the King dove in front of him.

The spell hit his shiny armor and bounced back toward the Fairy Godmother. When it hit, she exploded. All that was left were her glasses.

A small frog jumped out of the King's crown. "Ribbit," he croaked.

"Fiona," the frog said, "I'd hoped you'd never see me like this."

"Man, and he gave you a hard time," Donkey sneered.

"I only wanted what was best for Fiona," said the King. He looked at Shrek and his daughter. "But I can see that she already has it."

Shrek nodded. All was forgiven.

The castle clock started to chime. It was midnight.

"Midnight!?" Shrek realized. "Fiona, kiss me right now and we'll stay this way forever!"

Fiona smiled. "I'm happy with the man I married. I want him back."

The clock finished. Midnight had come and gone. No kiss. Shrek and Fiona held each other, unsure what might happen next. Their bodies shook and shimmied as the transformation began, turning them back into their ogre selves again.

"Now where was I," Shrek said thoughtfully. "Oh yes . . . " He dipped Fiona and kissed her. The crowd broke into applause and cheers.

Donkey ran up to the happy couple. He was back to his old Donkey self, too. After a huge fiesta at the castle, they all lived happily ever after. Really.

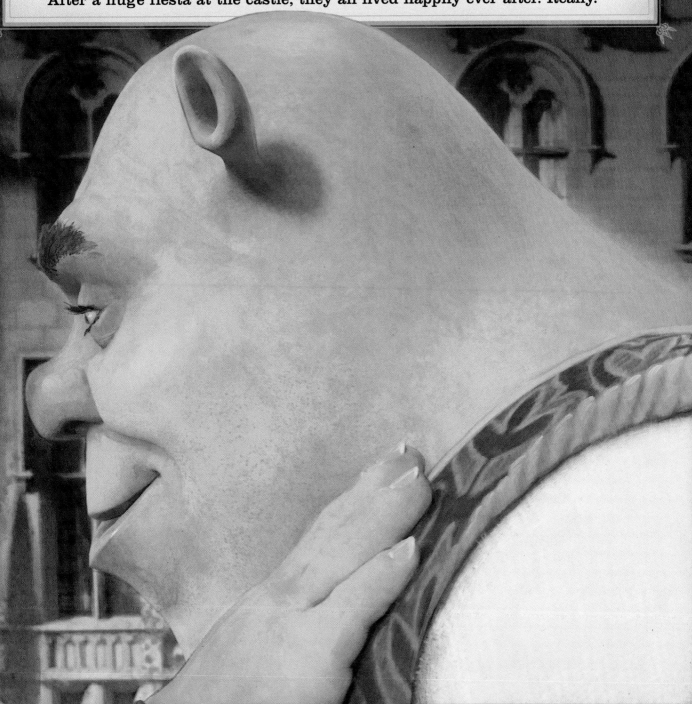